Goodnight Goodnight
SLEEPYHEAD

Originally published as *Eyes Nose Fingers Toes*

by *Ruth Krauss*

Illustrated by *Jane Dyer*

HarperCollins Publishers

Library of Congress Cataloging-in-Publication Data
Krauss, Ruth.   Goodnight goodnight sleepyhead / by Ruth Krauss ; illustrated by Jane Dyer.
p.   cm.   Text originally published under title: Eyes nose fingers toes: New York : Harper & Row, 1964.
Summary: In simple rhyming text, a child says goodnight to the things around her.
ISBN 0-06-028894-9 - ISBN 0-06-028895-7 (lib. bdg.)
[1. Bedtime-Fiction. 2. Stories in rhyme.] I. Dyer, Jane, ill.
II. Krauss, Ruth. Eyes nose fingers toes. III. Title.
PZ8.3.K865Go 2004   [E]-dc21   2003050805
Typography by Carla Weise
1 2 3 4 5 6 7 8 9 10
❖
First Edition

For my grandniece, Delaney Ann Reimer
—J.D.

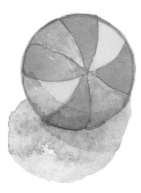

Eyes nose
fingers toes
lips hair...

everywhere

Goodnight eyes

Goodnight nose

Goodnight fingers

Goodnight toes

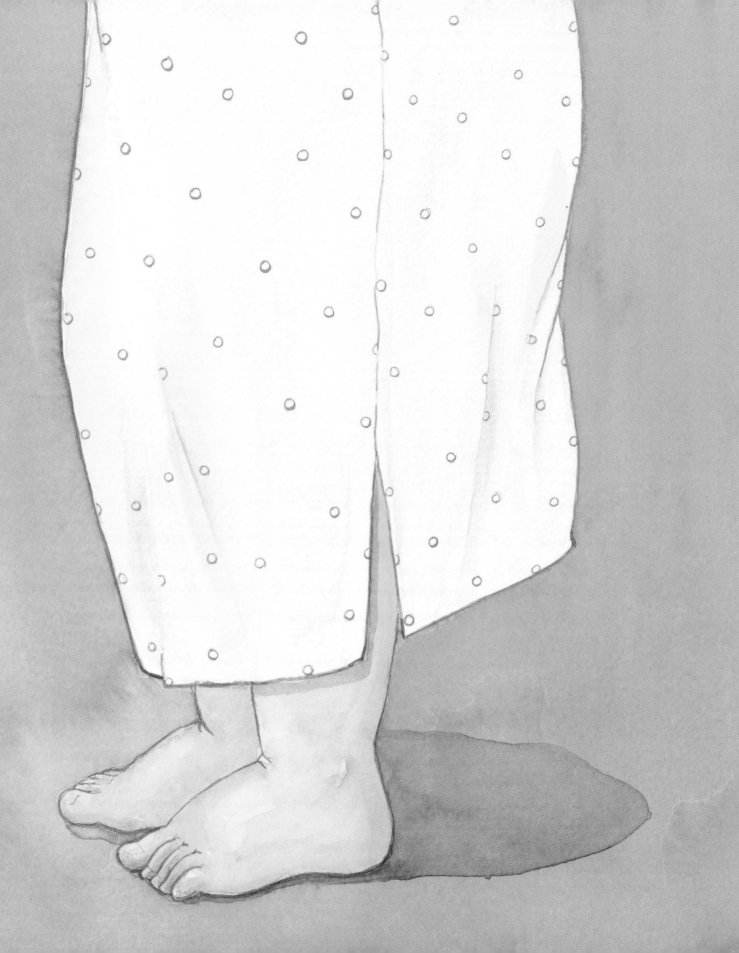

Goodnight lips

Goodnight hair

Goodnight Goodnight Everywhere

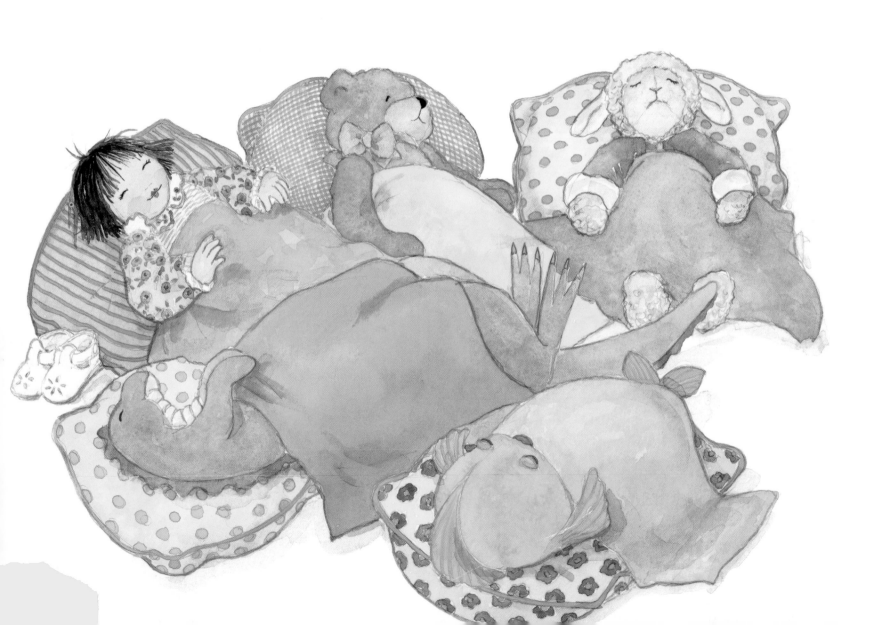

Goodnight windows

Goodnight doors

Goodnight walls

Goodnight floors

Goodnight chairs

Goodnight bed

Goodnight Goodnight
Sleepyhead

eyes nose fingers toes
lips hair everywhere
windows doors walls floors
chairs bed sleepyhead